In Need of Tinder

Written by
Noel Long

Illustrated by
Micaela Stefano

First edition, 2023

Geldmaker Publications, Dublin, Ireland

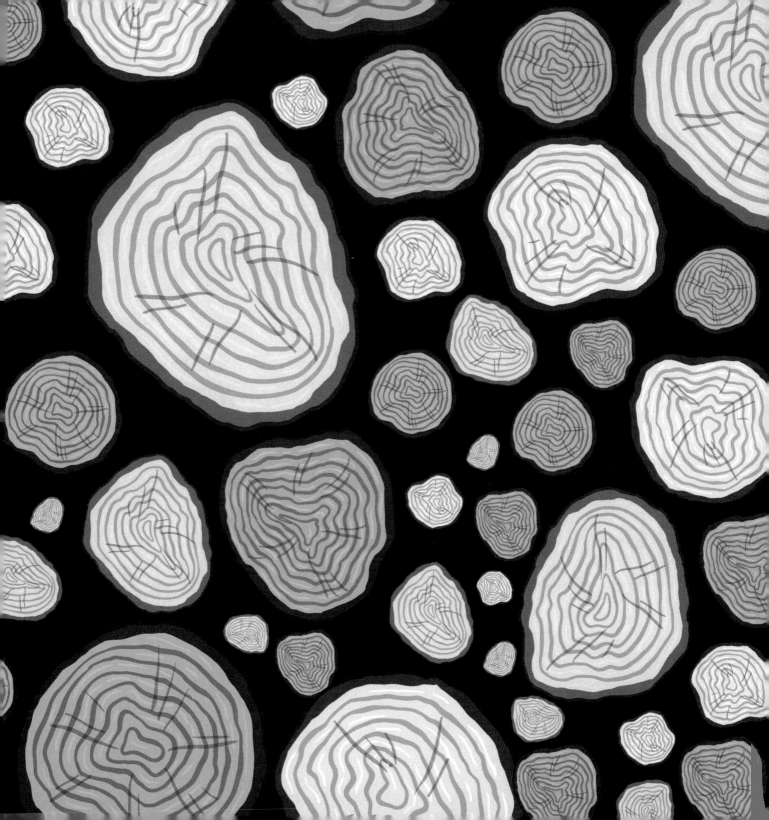

Mom's in need of tinder,
For this cold spell,
When she hasn't got any,
You can easily tell.

1

She has often wondered why,

It's so difficult to get a supply nearby...

Of perfectly good,

Reliable wood.

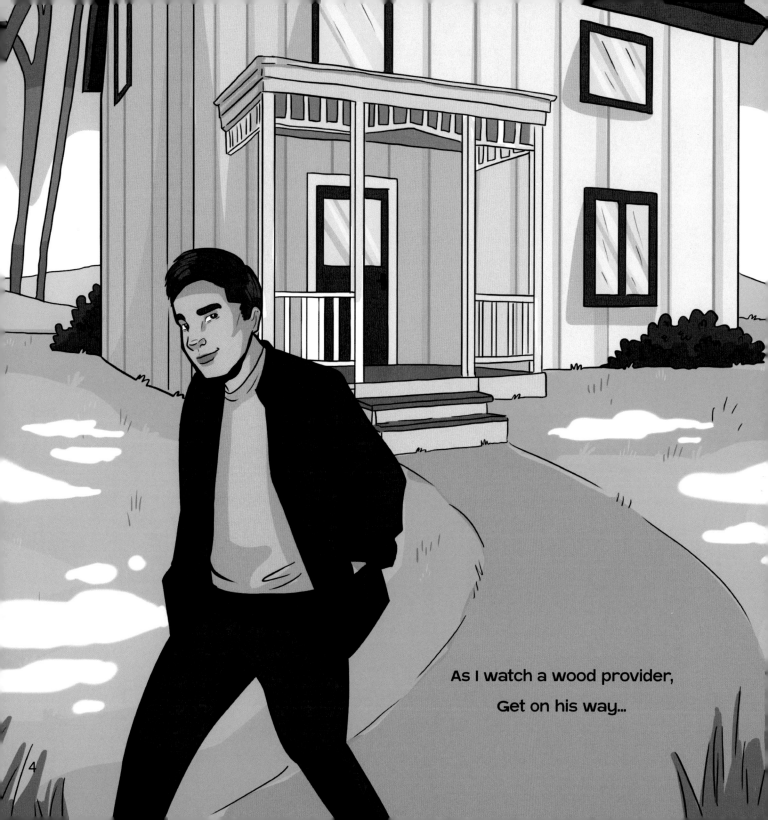

As I watch a wood provider,

Get on his way...

4

wood that's so good

Hitting the road,
After emptying his load.

5

"Thank God for tinder,"
I've often heard mom loudly moan,
She clearly loves having,
A warm home.

6

Most wood suppliers,
Tend to just unload and leave,
Except for faithful Steve,
Who has told mom she's pretty,
And played with her kitty.

Steve often waits around,
To eat a peach,
Later, on the phone,
He can easily be reached...

Should mom wish to chat,
There aren't many guys around,
Who are like that.

9

Could Steve be the dad,

That I never had?

He seems much nicer than,

Big, bad Brad...

Who was also a lumberjack,
He used to receive Mom's messages,
And never text back...
His heart was so black.

There's a lot of action,
In the woodshed.

14

Steve gets the job done quickly,
With my mom's help,
It wouldn't be as pleasurable,
Doing it by himself.

15

The man warming her home,
And heart this winter,
Is not a marathon runner,
But a sprinter.

If my mom is anything to go by,
Women shouldn't wait,
There could be great,
Tinder opportunities nearby.

Made in United States
Orlando, FL
26 November 2023